PAUL SIMON

THEMES AND VARIATIONS

TRUMPET

Arranged by
MARCEL ROBINSON

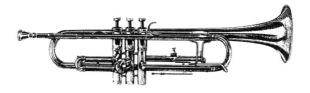

AMSCO PUBLICATIONS
New York/London/Sydney

Exclusive Distributors:
MUSIC SALES CORPORATION
24 East 22nd Street
New York, NY 10010 USA

MUSIC SALES LIMITED
8/9 Frith Street
London W1V 5TZ England

MUSIC SALES PTY. LIMITED
120 Rothschild Street
Rosebery, Sydney, NSW 2018, Australia

US International Standard Book Number: 0.8256.2555.6
UK International Standard Book Number: 0.7119.1513.X

Printed in the United States of America by
Vicks Lithograph and Printing Corporation

CONTENTS

PIANO ACCOMPANIMENT

The Boxer
Paul Simon

THEME
Moderately

Cecilia

Paul Simon

American Tune

Paul Simon

Mother And Child Reunion

Paul Simon

10

PULL-OUT PIANO ACCOMPANIMENTS

PAUL SIMON
THEMES AND VARIATIONS
TRUMPET

PAUL SIMON

THEMES AND VARIATIONS

TRUMPET

Arranged by
MARCEL ROBINSON

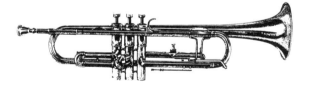

AMSCO PUBLICATIONS
New York/London/Sydney

The Boxer

Paul Simon

Cecilia

Paul Simon

American Tune

Paul Simon

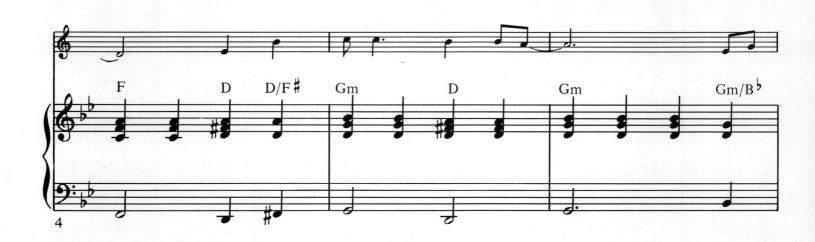

Mother And Child Reunion

Paul Simon

Duncan

Paul Simon

10

El Condor Pasa (If I Could)

Paul Simon, Jorge Milchberg and Daniel Robles

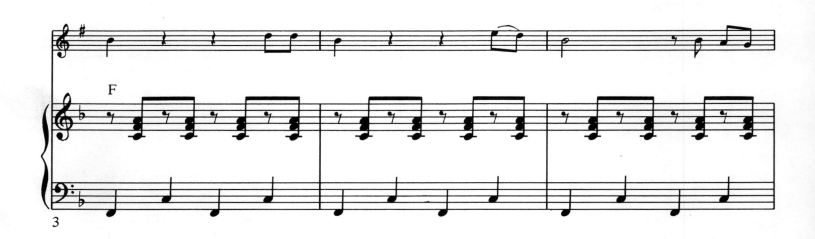

Fifty Ways To Leave Your Lover

Paul Simon

11

Duncan

Paul Simon

THEME
Moderately

Variation 1

Variation 2

Variation 3

El Condor Pasa (If I Could)

Paul Simon, Jorge Milchberg and Daniel Robles

THEME
Slowly

Variation 1

15

Variation 2

16

Fifty Ways To Leave Your Lover

Paul Simon

Variation 3

20